Unicorn Princesses

FIREFLY'S GLOW

P9-CEB-050

The Unicorn Princesses series

Unicorn Princesses

FIREFLY'S GLOW

Emily Bliss

illustrated by Sydney Hanson

BLOOMSBURY
CHILDREN'S BOOKS

NEW YORK LONDON OXFORD NEW DELHI SYDNEY

BLOOMSBURY CHILDREN'S BOOKS
Bloomsbury Publishing Inc., part of Bloomsbury Publishing Plc
1385 Broadway, New York, NY 10018

BLOOMSBURY, BLOOMSBURY CHILDREN'S BOOKS, and the Diana logo
are trademarks of Bloomsbury Publishing Plc

First published in the United States of America in August 2018
by Bloomsbury Children's Books
www.bloomsbury.com

Text copyright © 2018 by Emily Bliss
Illustrations copyright © 2018 by Sydney Hanson

All rights reserved. No part of this book may be reproduced or transmitted in any form
or by any means, electronic or mechanical, including photocopying, recording, or by any
information storage and retrieval system, without permission in writing from the publisher.

Bloomsbury books may be purchased for business or promotional use. For information on
bulk purchases please contact Macmillan Corporate and Premium Sales Department at
specialmarkets@macmillan.com

Library of Congress Cataloging-in-Publication Data
available upon request
ISBN 978-1-68119-926-9 (paperback) • ISBN 978-1-68119-927-6 (hardcover)
ISBN 978-1-68119-928-3 (e-book)

Book design by Jessie Gang and John Candell
Typeset by Westchester Publishing Services
Printed and bound in the U.S.A. by Berryville Graphics Inc., Berryville, Virginia
2 4 6 8 10 9 7 5 3   (paperback)
2 4 6 8 10 9 7 5 3 1 (hardcover)

All papers used by Bloomsbury Publishing, Inc., are natural, recyclable products
made from wood grown in well-managed forests. The manufacturing processes
conform to the environmental regulations of the country of origin.

To find out more about our authors and books visit www.bloomsbury.com
and sign up for our newsletters.

For Phoenix and Lynx

Unicorn Princesses
FIREFLY'S GLOW

Chapter One

In the top tower of Spiral Palace, Ernest, a wizard-lizard, sat at his desk. He adjusted his pointy purple hat. He straightened his cloak. And then he picked up a large black book with the title *Spells for Fruitmobiles: From Grape Go-Carts to Mango Motorcycles*. He flipped to the last page, where he found a spell that began, "Extremely Advanced (Only for

Very Experienced and Very Skilled Wizard-Lizards): Transforming Household Hooks into Plum Cars." Next to the spell was a picture of a grinning wizard-lizard speeding along in a six-wheeled sports car made out of three giant plums.

"Well," he said to himself, "Mother Lizard always did encourage me to challenge myself."

He studied the spell, whispering the words, "Vroomity Proomity Verity Prive! Make these Hooks into Plums that Drive!" over and over again. Then he pulled a screwdriver from his desk drawer and marched across the room to where three spare wizard's cloaks hung on three gold hooks.

bolts of orange lightning tear across the sky.

"Oh dear! Oh dear!" Ernest said. "I've done it again!" He reread the spell and grimaced. "I must have been so excited for Firefly's new library that I said the wrong thing. Hopefully she won't notice anything amiss." He sighed. And then he smiled to himself and added, "But I still really do want to drive a plum car!"

He read through the spell again. He lifted his wand. He opened his mouth. But before he could say, "Vroomity," six more orange lightning bolts flashed, and thunder boomed so loudly the hooks rattled against his desktop.

Ernest paused. He grimaced. "On second thought, maybe I'd better try something else," he said. Then he walked over to his shelf and pulled out a book titled *Magic Bags and Enchanted Luggage: Easy Spells for Beginners.*

Chapter Two

In the library at Pinewood Elementary School, Cressida Jenkins stood in front of the shelf with all the books about unicorns. There were twelve books total. She had read every single one at least twice. She had read five of them three times. And there were her two favorites—*An Illustrated Guide to Forest Unicorns* and *The Unicorn Encyclopedia*—that she had checked out and read cover-to-cover six times.

Cressida pulled *The Unicorn Encyclopedia* off the shelf. It had been a few weeks since she last read it, and she wanted to look at

her favorite picture: a giant, fold-out portrait of an orange, sparkling unicorn that reminded her of her friend, Princess Firefly. Cressida sat down on the library's blue carpet and flipped to page 17. She opened the flaps and smiled as she looked at the unicorn, who resembled Firefly in every way except that the unicorn in the book wasn't wearing a black ribbon necklace with a magic orange citrine gemstone.

Cressida loved the unicorn books in her school library, but she found herself wishing, right then, that there was a book all about the Rainbow Realm—a secret, magical world ruled by her friends, the unicorn princesses. How wonderful it would be, she thought, to open a book and see pictures of yellow Princess Sunbeam, silver Princess Flash, green Princess Bloom, purple Princess Prism, blue Princess Breeze, black Princess Moon, and orange Princess

Firefly. As she listed the unicorns' colors in her head, she paused. Why, she wondered, wasn't there a pink unicorn in the Rainbow Realm? And, for that matter, why wasn't there a unicorn that could fly?

That's when she had an idea that made her stand up and hop with excitement right there in the middle of the library. The second she got home from school, she would start writing and illustrating her very own book about the Rainbow Realm. And not only would she include the unicorns she already knew, but she would draw and write about a new pink flying unicorn too. Now she just needed to think of a name. Maybe Star or Sky or Wings or—

Ms. Wilcox, the school librarian, clapped

her hands three times. "It's time to check out your books and return to your classroom," she said.

Cressida closed *The Unicorn Encyclopedia* and stood up. As she walked through a maze of shelves toward the front desk, she kept imagining her book. Maybe the first page would be a giant picture of Spiral Palace, the unicorns' horn-shaped home. And after that—

"Cressida, are you ready to check out that book?" Ms. Wilcox asked.

Cressida had been so caught up in her plans that she hadn't even noticed she was standing right in front of Ms. Wilcox's desk.

"Yes, please," Cressida said, smiling

and handing Ms. Wilcox *The Unicorn Encyclopedia.*

"You had the biggest grin I think I've ever seen on anyone's face just now," Ms. Wilcox said. "What were you thinking about?"

Cressida never told adults—even kind adults like Ms. Wilcox—about the Rainbow Realm. Adults never seemed to understand that unicorns were real, and Cressida knew they would think she had simply imagined the unicorn princesses. "I was thinking about writing my own book," Cressida said.

"Well, that's a lovely idea," Ms. Wilcox said, and she stamped the page in the back of *The Unicorn Encyclopedia.*

"Thank you," Cressida said. And then she joined her friends Gillian and Eleanor as they lined up by the library door.

👑

When Cressida got home from school, she dropped her pink unicorn backpack by the front door and dashed into the kitchen, where she grabbed a chocolate-chip granola bar and a glass of water. She walked down the hall to her bedroom as fast as she could without spilling her drink. She closed the door so her older brother, Corey, wouldn't disturb her. And then she pulled a drawing pad and a box of art supplies from her closet and set them out on her desktop.

She could already see the cover of her

book in her head. The title, *The Rainbow Realm*, would be in big letters across the front. And then, underneath, she would draw a picture of all the unicorn princesses, including the pink one she had just invented, standing together in front of Spiral Palace. Under the picture, in smaller letters, she would write, "by Cressida Jenkins."

The first thing Cressida wanted to do, even before she drew the cover, was to find a way to make a book from several blank pieces of paper. Maybe, she thought, she could try folding a stack of paper in half and then stapling it together along the crease. But just as she began to rummage around in her art supplies box for a stapler, she heard a high, tinkling noise.

Cressida froze, and her heart skipped a beat with excitement. The high, tinkling noise grew louder, and Cressida leaped over to her bedside table, opened the drawer, and pulled out an old-fashioned key with a crystal ball handle that hummed and glowed bright pink. The key had been a gift from the unicorn princesses so that Cressida could visit the Rainbow Realm any time she wanted: all she had to do was push the key into a tiny hole in the base of an oak tree in the woods behind her house. The unicorn princesses had also told her that when they wanted to invite her to the Rainbow Realm for a special occasion, they would make the key's handle glow bright pink—just the way it was glowing right then!

At that moment, the only thing that sounded more fun to Cressida than writing a book about the Rainbow Realm was visiting the Rainbow Realm. She pushed the key into the back pocket of her jeans. She looked down to make sure her shirt—an orange top with a yellow, glittery firefly design on the front—didn't have any large grape-juice or tomato-sauce stains from lunch. She had been in such a hurry to start her book project that she hadn't even taken off her shoes: silver unicorn sneakers with bright pink lights that blinked every time she walked, jumped, or ran. She finished her water in three giant gulps and ate her granola bar in two huge bites. And then she ran out of her room and down the hall to the living room, where her mother sat reading a book and drinking coffee.

"I'm going for a quick walk in the woods," Cressida said as she sprinted to the back door. Time in the human world froze while Cressida was in the Rainbow Realm, so even if Cressida stayed with the unicorn princesses for hours, her mother would think she had been gone only a few minutes.

"Have a great time," her mother said.

Cressida sprinted across her back yard and into the woods. With her sneakers blinking, she ran along the path that led to the magic oak tree. When she got there, she pulled the key from her back pocket, kneeled at the tree's base, and pushed the key into a tiny hole.

Suddenly, the woods began to spin into a blur of green leaves, blue sky, and brown tree trunks. Then everything went pitch black, and Cressida had the sensation of falling fast through space. After several seconds, Cressida landed on something soft, and all she could see was a dizzying swirl of silver, white, pink, and purple. Soon the spinning slowed to a stop, and Cressida knew exactly where she was: sitting on a gigantic pink velvet armchair in the front hall of Spiral Palace.

Light from the sparkling crystal chandeliers reflected on the shiny white marble floors. Pink and purple curtains fluttered in the breeze. All around her were large pink and purple velvet couches and arm-chairs and silver troughs filled with water and honey. And across the room, all seven unicorn princesses stood in a tight circle, staring at something on the floor.

Chapter Three

From her armchair, Cressida leaned forward, then to her left, and then to her right, trying to catch a glimpse of what Sunbeam, Flash, Bloom, Prism, Breeze, Moon, and Firefly found so fascinating. It was, Cressida could see, a large book.

For a few seconds, Cressida watched her friends, not wanting to disturb them. After

all, she didn't like it when her mother, her father, or Corey interrupted her when she was reading. But she was also eager to say hello and to find out why the unicorn princesses had invited her to the Rainbow Realm.

When Cressida felt too excited and curious to wait any longer, she stood up and cleared her throat. None of the unicorns even twitched their ears or cocked their heads. Not wanting to startle her friends, Cressida whispered, "Hello." The unicorns still didn't notice her. Finally, in a loud voice, Cressida said, "I'm here!"

All seven unicorn princesses jumped straight up into the air. They turned toward Cressida. And then they burst out laughing.

"I'm sorry to surprise you!" Cressida said. "But I'm awfully glad to see you again."

"My human girl is back!" Sunbeam sang out as she danced over to Cressida.

"Welcome!" Flash said, galloping over.

Bloom and Prism trotted over and said at the same time, "We were hoping you would come!"

Moon winked and grinned.

Breeze, who looked like she had been sleeping, yawned and smiled groggily before she ambled toward Cressida.

"Cressida!" Firefly called out. "I'm thrilled you're here! We were so interested in this new book about musical instruments that we didn't even hear you arrive."

"Some of us were more interested than others," Breeze said, sighing. "I think I just fell asleep standing up." Her face brightened. "But now that Cressida's here, I'm happy to be awake!"

Firefly used her mouth and hooves to close the book. "We can finish this one later," she said to her sisters. She raced over to Cressida and gushed, "Today is the grand opening of the Rainbow Realm's very first library. And it's in my domain, the Shimmering Caves. Will you join us for the celebration? It's going to be a reading party, and all the creatures from the Rainbow Realm are invited!"

Cressida giggled. She had never seen Firefly so excited. "Absolutely," she said. "I didn't even know that unicorns like to read."

"Unicorns love to read," Firefly said, hopping back and forth. "It's one of our very favorite things to do!"

Sunbeam, Flash, Bloom, Prism, and Moon nodded in agreement. But Breeze frowned and snorted.

"My favorite books are about gardening," Bloom said. "I especially like stories about plants."

"I like books about painting and famous artists," Prism said.

"I like to read about sports," Flash said.

"I like to read about new games to play," Sunbeam said.

"I could read fiction all day long," Moon said. "I especially like books about dragons, phoenixes, and other magical creatures."

"But," Flash explained, "none of us likes to read as much as Firefly. She reads anything and everything. I've even caught her reading the dictionary."

Firefly beamed with pride. "It's true. I try to read at least four books every week. And I've read the dictionary, cover-to-cover, twice." She looked at Cressida and asked, "What do you like to read?"

Cressida grinned, thinking of the shelf of unicorn books at her school library. "I mostly like to read books about unicorns. And right before I came to visit you today, I was writing and illustrating my very own book, all about the Rainbow Realm."

"Amazing!" Firefly said, looking surprised and delighted by the idea. "Maybe, when you're finished, we could keep it in our new library."

Cressida grinned. "I would love that!" she said, imagining how much fun it would be to show her book to the unicorn princesses.

Just then, Cressida heard a loud sighing noise. She turned and saw that Breeze was standing apart from everyone else and staring at her hooves. "What's wrong?"

Cressida asked gently. "Are there kinds of books you like to read, too?"

"The truth is," Breeze said, "I don't like reading as much as my sisters. I like it for a little while, especially if the book is about exploring nature. But after a while, I get bored and fall asleep. Or I need to take a break from reading and do something outside, like flying a kite or going on a hike."

"I can completely understand that," Cressida said. While she was usually happy to curl up with a book, there were definitely times she would rather play tag or dance or climb trees. And if there was one thing she hated, it was sitting still when she felt like moving.

"I bet you'd like reading more if you just did it more often," Firefly said. "Reading is a habit you have to get into."

"Here they go again," Sunbeam whispered to Flash.

Flash nodded and whispered back, "No one is ever going to win this argument."

Bloom, Prism, and Moon exchanged worried looks.

Breeze's eyes flashed with anger. "Why don't you ever listen to me when I tell you I just don't like reading as much as the rest of you?" She stomped her hooves. "You know what?" Breeze continued, looking like she might start crying. "I don't even want to come to your library's grand opening party. The last place I want to be is in a room full of books with everyone spending hours and hours reading and talking about how much they love reading. That is not my idea of a fun party." And with that, she turned and galloped away, disappearing down the hall.

Firefly's face fell. "I always say the wrong thing to Breeze whenever we talk about books. I try to be encouraging, but I just seem to make her angrier."

Sunbeam and Flash nodded in agreement.

"Bloom and I have even tried reading out loud to her," Prism said.

"I lent her my favorite book of stories, but she gave it back after she'd only read the first chapter," Moon said.

Firefly frowned. "It will ruin the grand

opening party if Breeze isn't there. I've been looking forward to this afternoon for months. And now the whole thing might fall apart."

"Don't worry, Firefly," Moon said. "I'm pretty sure I can convince Breeze to come to the party. I know she loves putting up decorations. How about if she and I come a little early to help you hang up balloons and streamers? That might put her in a better mood."

Firefly took a deep breath. "Thank you," she said. "That would be amazing." Then Firefly's excited grin returned to her face. She looked at Cressida and asked, "Want to come help me put the final touches on the new library? There are a few more books I need to put on the shelves."

"Absolutely!" Cressida said.

Firefly kneeled so Cressida could climb onto her back. But just then, a high, nasal voice that was unmistakably Ernest's called out, "Wait! Don't go quite yet!"

The wizard-lizard sprinted into the room, out of breath. "Just one thing," he said, panting, "before you go!"

"Hello, Ernest," Cressida said, giggling.

"I've got a present for Cressida," Ernest said. "I've been practicing for the past two hours, and I've gotten this spell to work perfectly, one hundred percent of the time.

Not a single hitch!" He paused and blushed. "Well, maybe a hitch or two. Or even three. But, um, I know I'll get it right this time."

Cressida giggled.

Ernest pulled his wand from his cloak pocket and waved it as he chanted, "Bookily Snookily Readily Rack! Please Make Cressida an Orange Quack Stack!"

Wind swirled around Cressida. And then, right in front of her was a tower of bright orange ducks. "Quack! Quack! Quack!" the ducks called out, opening their orange beaks and blinking. They looked, Cressida thought, very confused.

"Oh dear!" Ernest said, scratching his forehead. "Did I say 'quack stack' again?

There are ducks all over my room at the moment. Let me give it another go."

He raised his wand and chanted, "Quackily Quickily Quirkily Quond! Please send the quack stack straight back to the pond. Bookily Snookily Readily Rack! Please Make Cressida a Magic Backpack!"

Another gust of wind swirled around Cressida. The ducks vanished. And then, in her hands appeared a glittery orange backpack with rainbow-striped straps. Shiny orange gems—just like the magic citrine on Firefly's black ribbon necklace— spelled "CRESSIDA" across the outer compartment.

"I love it!" Cressida said, grinning. "It's the perfect size for books!"

"That's exactly what I was thinking," Ernest said.

"Thank you, Ernest," Cressida said.

Ernest took a bow.

And then Cressida heard what sounded like at least a hundred ducks quacking in another part of the palace.

"Oh dear!" Ernest said. "I bet they're hungry again. Off I go to feed the ducks!"

And with that, he turned on his back claws and sprinted down the hall.

Cressida put on the backpack and twirled around. "What do you think?" she asked Firefly.

"You look ready to go spelunking," Firefly said, grinning.

"Spelunking?" Cressida said, enjoying the sound of the strange, new word as she said it. "What is that?"

"Spelunking means 'exploring caves.' I learned it the last time I read the dictionary," Firefly said.

"Well," Cressida said, "I'm definitely ready for spelunking!"

Firefly kneeled, and Cressida climbed onto her back.

"See you at the Glow Library!" Firefly said as she trotted across the front hall of Spiral Palace.

"See you soon!" Sunbeam and Flash said.

"We can't wait to see the library!" Bloom and Prism said.

"I'll aim to get there with Breeze half an hour early!" Moon called out as Firefly leaped out the palace's front door.

Chapter Four

As Firefly galloped along the clear stones that led from Spiral Palace to the surrounding forest, Cressida held on tightly to the unicorn's silky orange mane. For a few seconds, Cressida glanced back to admire the princesses' sparkling home. She giggled when she spotted an entire flock of orange ducks sitting on the roof of the palace's top tower. She faced forward again as Firefly turned onto a thin trail that wound downhill through a grove of cedar trees.

Cressida inhaled and smiled. She loved the smell of cedar.

"I absolutely can't wait to show you the Shimmering Caves," Firefly said. "And I'm even more excited to show you the Glow Library. I've been working on it for months. There's a huge reading chair for each of my sisters and me. And I made sure to include all the different kinds of books my sisters like. They'll love it! Well," she added, sounding worried, "all of them but Breeze will love it. If you can think of any way to make Breeze like the library a little more, will you let me know?"

"The library sounds amazing," Cressida said. "I can't wait to see it."

Cressida remembered what Breeze had said about not liking reading as much as her sisters. There were certainly some activities, like swimming, that Cressida didn't like quite as much as her friends did. Cressida could swim just fine, and she enjoyed playing in the water for an hour or two. But when she went to the pool with Eleanor and Gillian, she always wanted to leave before they did. There had been a few times when her friends had tried to convince her to like swimming more, and when that happened, Cressida had ended up liking swimming even less. She guessed that was how Breeze felt.

"It's so very kind of you to try to think of a way to make your new library more appealing to Breeze," Cressida said gently to Firefly. "It might be that Breeze won't ever like reading quite as much as you do. I know this sounds like a strange idea, but if you accept that about her and don't try to change her mind, she might be more willing to do reading activities with you and your sisters."

"Really?" Firefly asked.

"I was just thinking that I usually like things even less when my friends try to make me like them more," Cressida said.

Firefly was quiet for several seconds. "Now that I think about it, that's how I am too," she said. "The more Bloom tries to get me to like gardening, the more I don't even want to try weeding or planting seeds. But probably if she'd stop trying to convince me that gardening is as much fun as reading, I'd be glad to occasionally help her with the Enchanted Garden."

"I can completely understand that," Cressida said. "I'm the same way with swimming."

"I'd better think about it a little more," Firefly said. She slowed down, and the path entered a clearing with large gray rocks and small hills covered in long grass. She trotted down a steep, rocky path and stopped in front of a hill with a shiny orange door built right into it. Above the door was a black sign that said "Shimmering Caves" in glittery citrine gems. "Are you ready?" Firefly asked, kneeling down.

"Yes!" Cressida said, and she slid off Firefly's back.

Firefly hopped back and forth on her hooves with excitement. "Let's go spelunking!" she said, and she used her mouth to pull open the door.

Cressida followed Firefly into a narrow corridor made of stone. Torches mounted on the walls overflowed with blinking fireflies. Lanterns brimming with glow-in-the-dark rocks hung from the ceiling. Tiny flecks of citrine embedded in the stone walls and ceiling shimmered in the pale yellow light.

"This is amazing!" Cressida said.

"I was hoping you'd like it," Firefly said. "We have time for a little fun before we finish getting ready for the reading party. My very favorite cave is the library. But do you want to see my second favorite?"

"Definitely!" Cressida said. She and Firefly walked farther along the corridor and then down a long spiral staircase made of giant slabs of glowing rock. At the bottom, Firefly and Cressida came to an orange door with a black sign above it that said "The Cave of Creativity" in pieces of citrine.

Firefly opened the door, and Cressida followed her into a large shimmering orange cavern. Stalactites hung down from the ceiling like long icicles, and stalagmites jutted up from the floor like thin towers that reminded Cressida of miniature models of Spiral Palace. Torches affixed to the cavern walls brimmed with fireflies, and the floor was made of glowing yellow rocks.

"You must be Cressida!" a voice called out.

Cressida turned toward the voice. A long, thin stalactite with bright eyes and a smiling mouth winked at her and said, "I'm Stella! Stella the stalactite."

"And I'm Stuart," a stalagmite said. "Princess Firefly has told us all about you."

"It's wonderful to meet you," Cressida said, giggling. "I've never met a stalactite or a stalagmite before."

"We've never met a human girl before," Stella and Stuart said.

And then all the stalactites and stalag-mites sang out, "Welcome, Cressida!" Their echoing voices sounded both eerie and beautiful, and goosebumps suddenly covered Cressida's arms.

"We're about to go put the finishing touches on the library," Firefly explained to the stalactites and stalagmites. "But first, I was thinking we could show Cressida the Cave of Creativity's special magic power."

"Fantastic idea!" the stalactites and sta-lagmites called out.

Firefly turned to Cressida and said, "Close your eyes and imagine the cover of a book you'd like to read this afternoon at the grand opening."

Cressida closed her eyes. For a moment,

her mind went blank. And then she remembered the pink flying unicorn she had made up in the library at school. That seemed like the perfect subject for a book to read at the grand opening party. She imagined what the cover would look like: a pink unicorn with a magic ruby gemstone necklace soaring high above pale pink clouds. As soon as the picture looked clear in her mind, Cressida heard a high, humming noise.

"You can look now," Firefly said.

Cressida opened her eyes. The stalactites and stalagmites began to flicker and flash in every color of the rainbow. The humming grew louder and more rhythmic. All the fireflies that had been in the torches joined together to form one gigantic yellow swarm that flew faster and faster in circles around the cave. After several seconds, the humming crescendoed and then grew softer and softer. The fireflies slowed down and then, in small groups, returned to the torches. The stalactites and stalagmites stopped flickering and flashing. Finally, a tiny door on the other side of the cave that Cressida hadn't even noticed before opened.

Five large yellow worms with curly orange hair and big fluorescent-green glasses emerged carrying a book. "Those are the bookworms," Firefly whispered to Cressida.

Grinning proudly, the bookworms slid across the cave until they were right in front of Cressida's silver unicorn sneakers.

"Proudly presenting *Adventures in the Air* for Cressida Jenkins," the bookworms said in unison. They smiled as Cressida kneeled down and picked up the book, which felt warm, like clothes that had just come out of the dryer. The cover looked exactly like the one she had imagined, only better: the unicorn was an even brighter shade of pink, the clouds looked even softer and puffier, and the ruby on the unicorn's neck-lace looked even shinier.

"Thank you!" Cressida said to the bookworms.

"Our pleasure!" they said. And then they turned around, slid across the cave floor, and disappeared behind the tiny door.

Cressida stood up and showed the book to Firefly. "I can't wait to read it!" she said.

Firefly looked at the cover, and her eyes widened in surprise. "You imagined a book about my sister!" she said.

"Your sister?" Cressida said.

"Oh, you've never met Feather!" Firefly said, smiling. "She's the second youngest unicorn princess. Her magic power is to fly, and she's very adventurous. She's been away from Spiral Palace for a long time, exploring far-off realms and meeting other magical creatures."

Cressida grinned. She loved the idea that there really was another unicorn princess— especially one that was pink and could fly. "Maybe I could meet her the next time she comes back to the Rainbow Realm," Cressida said.

"What a fantastic idea," Firefly said. "We'll be sure to invite you to visit us as soon as she comes home."

"Thank you," Cressida said.

Firefly looked again at *Adventures in the Air* and said, "That book looks so good I'd love to start reading it with you right now. But I think we'd better go finish getting the library ready. We'll have plenty of time to read it at the grand opening party."

"That sounds great," Cressida said as she put the book inside her backpack.

"Thank you so much for visiting us!" Stella called out.

"Yes, come back any time!" Stuart chimed in.

"See you soon, Cressida," all the stalactites and stalagmites sang out. Echoing laughter filled the cave, and Cressida giggled as even more goosebumps covered her arms.

"It was wonderful to meet you. Thank you so much for the book!" she called out as she followed Firefly out the door.

Chapter Five

A nd now, I can't wait to show you Glow Library!" Firefly gushed as she led Cressida down another narrow corridor. "I've spent every morning for the past six months in the Cave of Creativity imagining all the books to fill the shelves. And after that, I organized all the books so it would be easy for my sisters and me to find exactly the kinds of books we feel like reading. There are a few more books I want to put on the shelves. And maybe you can tell me if you think I put the armchairs in the right places."

Cressida was so excited to see the library that she could barely keep herself from jumping and dancing alongside Firefly.

Firefly stopped in front of an orange door. Above it, in orange gems, a sign read, "WELCOME TO THE GLOW LIBRARY."

Firefly pulled the door open. And then she gasped. "Oh no!" she whispered. Cressida opened her eyes and blinked with surprise at the scene in front of her.

The cave looked like it would have been

an incredible library. Floor-to-ceiling shelves covered all the walls. Grand chandeliers crowded with fireflies hung from the ceilings. Reading lamps, teeming with even more fireflies, bent over giant orange and yellow velvet armchairs that looked perfect for reading. Above each set of shelves was a sign made of glowing gems. There were more signs than Cressida could read all at once, but she noticed ones that said, "Fun and Games," "Sports," "Gardening and Plants," "Art and Artists," "The Great Outdoors," "Fiction," "Adventure," and "Magic."

The trouble, though, was that there were no books on any of the shelves. Instead, the

books were in messy heaps and towering piles all over the floor. But that wasn't the most surprising thing about what Cressida saw. Everywhere she looked, there were dozens and dozens of tiny magical creatures, each the size of Cressida's hand.

On the chairs, tiny unicorns dipped their mouths into bags labeled "SEEDS" and flung what looked like clouds of dust onto the cushions. Rainbow cats and gnomes darted around chair legs and across small piles of open books flying kites, playing hide-and-seek, and chasing each other in games of tag. Dragons wearing hats and scarves skied down the sides of mountains of books, while silver and gold foxes hiked to the peaks wearing bulging backpacks. On the floor, between the piles of books, phoenixes kicked balls back and forth and swung rackets with their beaks. On some of the shelves, painted fairies, unicorns, dragons, and phoenixes wearing smocks painted on easels and admired each other's artwork. On other shelves, unicorns ate from troughs, slept, walked, talked, and laughed. Cressida looked up to the ceiling and saw unicorns, wizard-lizards, trolls, and griffins floating in hot air balloons, hang gliding, and riding magic kites in loops around the chandeliers.

"What on earth do you think happened?" Firefly asked.

"I'm not sure," Cressida said, though she

was almost positive one of Ernest's magical mishaps was to blame.

For several more seconds she and Firefly stared at the miniature creatures.

"It's interesting to watch them," Firefly sniffled. "But my library is a disaster. I'll have to cancel the grand opening. And I worked so hard to imagine all these books and organize them. It took months and months of work. And now everything is ruined." Tears slid down Firefly's cheeks.

Cressida wrapped her arms around Firefly's neck. "I'm so sorry this happened," Cressida said. "But let's not cancel the grand opening just yet. There must be something we can do." As she said it, Cressida had to admit she had no idea how they could

possibly move so many miniature creatures, organize the books, and put them
back on the shelves before the party was
supposed to start.

Firefly took a deep breath. "You're
right," she said. "Let's see what we can do.
Maybe we should start by trying to move
all these creatures."

"Good idea," Cressida said.

Firefly cleared her throat and shouted,
"Excuse me, tiny magical creatures! Please
line up in front of me!"

The creatures didn't even look up.

"Would it work to pick them up?" Firefly asked.

"I could try it," Cressida said, feeling
a little nervous. She walked over to an

armchair where a unicorn was throwing seeds into the cushion. She slowly reached toward the unicorn, but the unicorn whinnied and reared up, looking frightened. "I'm sorry, little unicorn," Cressida whispered softly, and she pulled her hand away. The unicorn immediately resumed throwing seeds.

"Do you have any other ideas?" Firefly asked.

"Let me think for just a moment," Cressida said. She looked down at her feet, trying to imagine a creative way to herd dozens of creatures to a different part of the Shimmering Caves. And then something odd caught her eye: a book lay open on the floor, and though it had words on

the pages, there were two blank white rectangles where Cressida would have expected
to see illustrations. Cressida picked up the
book and turned the page. Again, there
were words and more blank white rectangles. She flipped through the book. There
was not a single picture or illustration.

She closed the book and looked at the
cover. *Winter Sports for Magical Creatures* was
written in cursive across the front, right
above another blank rectangle.

Cressida looked more closely at the biggest mountain of books. Not only were there dragons skiing down it, but there were trolls, unicorns, and fairies snowshoeing, cross-country skiing, riding sleds, and figure skating.

"That's interesting," Cressida said to herself. She picked up another book. The cover said *Painting Fruit: A Guide for Magical Creatures* above a large blank rectangle. She flipped through the book and, sure enough, there were words, but only blank squares and rectangles where the pictures should have been. Careful not to step on any of the creatures, Cressida walked around several heaps of books and over to the set of shelves where the fairies were painting at easels. She looked more closely. Fairies, unicorns, dragons, and phoenixes painted rainbows and landscapes on one shelf. On another, the magical creatures used pencils to sketch trolls and mermaids. And on the next shelf where Cressida looked, she found unicorns, phoenixes, and dragons wearing smocks and berets, painting pictures of the fruits Cressida had seen when she visited the Enchanted Garden with Bloom: roinkleberries, cranglenapples, and froyananas.

Cressida walked back over to Firefly. "I'm pretty sure," Cressida said, "that these tiny creatures are from the pictures in all these books."

"I thought they looked awfully familiar," Firefly said. Then her face fell. "But now the books are ruined too. Oh, what will we do?"

Suddenly Cressida had an idea. "I think I have a plan!" she said, jumping with excitement. "I'm not sure if it will work, but we won't know unless we try."

Firefly's face brightened. "Do you have magic powers you haven't told me about?" she asked with a playful smile.

"Possibly," Cressida said, winking at Firefly. "The first thing we need to do is go back to the Cave of Creativity."

"Let's go!" Firefly said, and the two dashed out of the library, down the corridor, and back into the cave with all the stalactites and stalagmites.

Chapter Six

As soon as Cressida and Firefly stepped into the Cave of Creativity, Stella called out, "Welcome back!"

"Do you need another book?" asked Stuart.

"It just so happens that I do," Cressida said.

"We're ready when you are," Stella

said. "Just shut your eyes and imagine the cover."

Cressida closed her eyes and imagined a book cover with a picture of a human girl casting a spell as she held a magic wand. The cave began to hum. Cressida opened her eyes and watched as the stalactites and stalagmites flickered and flashed and the fireflies left their torches to swarm in circles around the cave. The humming crescendoed. And then it faded as the stalactites and stalagmites stopped flashing and flickering and the fireflies returned to their torches. The tiny door on the other side of the cave opened, and out slid the bookworms, carrying a large, bright red book.

When they were right in front of Cressida's sneakers, the bookworms said, "Presenting *Spells for Human Girls and Boys*." They winked at Cressida as she kneeled and picked up the book.

"Thank you so very much," Cressida said, again feeling the warmth of the book's cover against her hands.

"Our pleasure," said the bookworms. And then they slid back across the cave and through their tiny door.

Cressida's heart quickened as she opened the book to the table of contents. There were spells to make fairy wings, flying broomsticks, and rocket-powered shoes. There were spells to turn dirt into chocolate, rocks into ice cream, and flowers into lollipops. Halfway down the list, Cressida found the title of exactly the spell she was looking for: "Returning Characters to Books, page 54." She jumped with excitement as she turned to page 54. Then she held the book so both she and Firefly could read the instructions:

Returning Characters to Books

ITEMS NEEDED:
1. Magic wand
2. Magic backpack
3. Citrine stones
4. Hair of worm
5. Hair of unicorn
6. Hair of girl

METHOD:

Combine items 3 through 6, above, in the bottom of the magic backpack (item 2) and zip it up. Wave your magic wand (item 1) over the backpack as you chant, "Hairily Glairily Glittery Glooks! Send these characters back to their books!" Then, sprinkle the magic dust you create over the characters.

"Hmm," Cressida said. "I don't have a magic wand. Do you?"

"No," Firefly said, frowning.

"Did I hear you say you need a magic wand?" Stella asked. Cressida looked up to see the stalactite smiling hopefully. "I'd be wand-shaped if you pulled me off this cave ceiling! And I would say I'm magic, too, given that I'm a talking stalactite that helps to magically create books."

"Would it hurt you if I pulled you off?" Cressida asked. She wasn't sure if a magic stalactite could be substituted for a magic wand, but it certainly wouldn't hurt to try.

"Not at all!" Stella said. "I've always wanted to try out freedom, at least for a little while. Just wrap your hands right below my mouth and pull."

Cressida walked over to Stella and put her hands on the bottom of the long, thin stalactite. She pulled gently, and to her amazement, Stella easily came off the ceiling.

"Whoa!" Stella said, as Cressida carried her over to Firefly. "This is wild! 'Stella the Wand' doesn't have quite the same ring to it as 'Stella the Stalactite,' but it sure is fun to try this out."

"Thanks so much for helping us out," Cressida said. She looked down at the open spell book. "Now we have a wand. And we have my magic backpack. It looks like next we need some citrines."

"I've still got some more of the ones I used to make all the signs in the library," Firefly said. "I'll be right back."

After Firefly bolted out the door, Cressida turned to Stella. "Do you think the worms might be willing to give us a strand or two of their wonderful curly hair?" she asked.

"I bet they would," Stella said. She called out, "Belinda? Any chance you could come help us out?"

The little door opened, and a bookworm slid out and said, "You called?"

"Is there any chance we could have a few strands of your hair?" Stella asked.

"Sure," Belinda said. "But someone else will have to pull it out." She smiled and winked. "I don't have any arms or hands, in case you didn't notice."

"I can do it very gently," Cressida said. She laid Stella down on the cave floor and kneeled in front of the bookworm. Then, as carefully as she could, she plucked one long, curly strand of hair from the worm's head.

"That didn't hurt a bit!" Belinda said. "Why don't you take another one, just in case you need two."

"Thank you," Cressida said, and she pulled out one more strand of hair.

"You're most welcome," Belinda said. "Not to be rude, but is that all you need? I'm happy to help in any way I can, but I was right in the middle of the best book I've ever read. I can't wait to get back to it."

Cressida laughed. "All done! Thank you so much for your help."

Cressida took off her backpack, un-zipped it, and pulled out her book. Then she dropped the two strands of Belinda's hair into the bottom of the pack just as Firefly returned holding a small orange velvet bag in her mouth. Cressida took the bag, and Firefly said, "Here are the citrine gemstones!" Cressida dumped the small orange jewel pieces into the backpack.

Then she quickly plucked two strands of her own dark hair and dropped them on top of the citrines and Belinda's hair.

Firefly looked into the backpack and then at the open spell book. She glanced nervously at Cressida. "Now all you need is my hair," she said, frowning. "Will it hurt when you pull it out?"

"I know what we could try that won't hurt at all," Cressida said. "Why don't you shake your head, and we can see if any of the hair in your mane falls out on its own."

Firefly's face brightened. "Great idea!" she said. She shook her head, and, sure enough, four silky orange hairs floated downward.

Cressida scooped them up and dropped them into the backpack. She zipped it up and picked up Stella. "Are you ready to be a magic wand?" she asked.

"Ready as I'll ever be," Stella laughed.

Cressida held Stella above the backpack, and, reading from the open spell book, she chanted, "Hairily Glairily Glittery Glooks! Send these Characters Back to their Books!"

A swirl of glowing light raced in circles around the backpack. Then there was a

loud *"Poof!"* Cressida and Firefly looked at each other with wide eyes. Cressida unzipped the backpack to find it filled with glittery yellow dust.

"Wow!" Firefly said. "I can't believe that worked!"

"Me neither," Cressida said. Then she

looked at Stella. "Are you ready to be a stalactite again?"

"Yes," Stella said. "It was fun being a magic wand. But I'm ready to hang from the ceiling again."

Cressida carefully pushed Stella up against the cave ceiling, and the stalactite magically reattached. "It's good to be home," Stella said, winking at Cressida and Firefly. "Good luck with your magic dust."

"Thank you," Cressida said.

"I can't wait to try this out," Firefly said. "Let's go!"

Cressida put on the backpack, which now felt as though it were filled with sand,

and picked up both of her new books. Then she and Firefly ran as fast as they could out of the Cave of Creativity, down the corridor, and back into the library.

Chapter Seven

When they stepped back into Glow Library, Cressida and Firefly paused for a few seconds to watch the tiny magical creatures as they played on the mountains of books. Then Cressida set her two books down on the floor and slid off her backpack. "Are you ready to send these creatures back into the books?" Cressida asked.

"Yes," Firefly said. "But I have to admit they're awfully fun to watch."

"I agree," Cressida said. She unzipped the backpack and grabbed a handful of glittery yellow magic dust. It felt, she thought, like the flour she used when she helped her father bake cookies and bread. Cressida sprinkled the dust on some rainbow cats, gnomes, and unicorns who were playing hopscotch, hide-and-seek, and tag right by her feet. Light swirled around the creatures. A book that lay on the floor glowed for a few seconds. Suddenly, the creatures vanished. Cressida picked up the book that had glowed and flipped it open. Sure enough, instead of blank rectangles, the book now had illustrations. She

paused at a page with a picture of a unicorn playing hopscotch. For one moment, the unicorn turned to Cressida and whispered, "Thank you! I'm so glad to be back home." The unicorn winked, turned toward her friend, and froze mid-jump.

"It worked!" Cressida said, jumping up and down.

"Amazing!" Firefly said.

Cressida walked through the room, sprinkling the magic dust on the miniature creatures. Again and again, a gold light swirled around the creatures, the books where they belonged glowed for several seconds, and then the creatures vanished.

When all the miniature creatures were finally back in their books, Firefly sighed in relief. "Thank you, Cressida," she said. "That was such a creative way to solve that problem." Firefly looked at all the messy heaps of books. "But I don't think there's any way we can organize and shelve all these books before the grand opening.

We'll still have to cancel the party." She blinked back more tears.

"I think I know how we can put the books back on the shelves quickly," Cressida said. "But we'll need help from Moon and Breeze."

Just then, Cressida heard the clatter of hooves coming down the corridor. She turned to see Moon and Breeze standing at the entrance to the library.

"Oh dear," Moon said, looking at the mess of books. "What happened?"

"You should have seen it before," Firefly said, and she told Moon and Breeze the story of how they'd found the library overrun with miniature magical creatures, and then how she and Cressida had magically transported the characters back to their books.

"That's amazing!" Moon said.

"But what about the grand opening party?" Breeze asked. "How will you organize and shelve all the books in time?"

"I have a plan," Cressida said, and she turned to Moon and Breeze. "But we'll need magical help from both of you."

"Of course!" Moon said.

Breeze frowned. She looked at Firefly. "I know you worked incredibly hard to create this library, and I'll definitely help you put all the books back. But I'm still not so sure about coming to the party. I'm really dreading it. I just don't like reading as much as the rest of you," she said. She glared at Firefly as though she were waiting for her sister to argue with her.

Firefly opened her mouth to say something. But then, she stopped. She glanced at Cressida. Cressida nodded encouragingly. Firefly turned back to Breeze and said, "I can completely understand that."

Breeze blinked in surprise. "You can?" she asked.

"Absolutely," Firefly said. "Everyone likes different things. I don't like flying kites and hiking as much as you do. And you don't like reading as much as I do. The Rainbow Realm would be an awfully boring place if we unicorn princesses were all exactly the same."

"That's definitely true," Breeze said.

Firefly stared down at her hooves for a few seconds. Then she looked back at Breeze. "I'm really sorry I've kept trying to convince you to like reading as much as I do. I shouldn't have done that. I think I just love reading so much that it's hard for me to understand that not everyone else feels the same way."

Breeze nodded. And then she smiled. "I forgive you," she said. "It's not that I hate reading or the library. It's just that there are other things I usually like to do more."

"That makes perfect sense," Firefly said. "I'll stop trying to change your mind."

Breeze smiled. "Well, in that case," she said, "not only am I happy to help in any way I can to clean up this mess, but I'd also be glad to come to the grand opening party, even if there's not enough time to put up decorations first. A reading party isn't my favorite thing in the world, but I can do it for an afternoon. And," she said, looking up at the signs above the sections, "maybe I'll even find a book I like in the Great Outdoors section."

"I made that section just for you," Firefly said. "But," she continued, winking at Breeze, "it's perfectly fine if you don't like the books in it quite as much as I do." Then Firefly leaned over to Cressida and whispered in her ear, "You were right. Breeze stopped hating reading when I stopped trying to make her like it."

Cressida smiled and nodded. Then she

looked at Moon, Breeze, and Firefly and said, "Are you ready to put all these books back?"

"Yes!" the three unicorns said all at once.

"Great!" Cressida said. "Moon, can you make the library pitch black?"

"Sure thing!" Moon said. Her opal shimmered and glittered. Sparkling light poured from her horn. And then the cave went pitch black.

Cressida felt a little nervous in the dark, and she reached out and put a hand on Firefly's neck. "Firefly," Cressida said, "can you make all the Fun and Games books glow in the dark?"

"Absolutely," Firefly said. Glittery

orange light shot from Firefly's horn, and then Cressida saw glowing books all around the room.

"Breeze," Cressida said, "can you make a magic gust of wind that will pick up all the glowing books and put them on the Fun and Games shelf?"

"Yes," Breeze said. In the dim light created by the glowing books, Cressida could see Breeze's aquamarine shimmer. Glittery blue light shot from her horn, and a comet-shaped gust of wind darted around the library. Soon all the glowing books lifted into the air, paraded in a circle overhead, and then slid, one by one, onto the set of shelves under the Fun and Games sign.

"It worked!" Cressida said. "Firefly, can

you make the Art and Artists books glow next?"

"Absolutely!" Firefly said. Glittery orange light poured from Firefly's horn. The books already on the shelves stopped glowing. For a moment, the library was pitch black. And then more of the books in heaps on the floor glowed.

"Now it's my turn again," Breeze said. Glittery blue light shot from her horn. Another gust of wind danced around the room, lifted the glowing books from the floor, and put them on the shelves under the Art and Artists sign.

Cressida, Firefly, and Breeze worked together to put the rest of the books back where they belonged, section by section.

When they were finished, Firefly said, "Moon, I think you can make it light in here again."

"Great!" Moon said. Sparkling light poured from her horn. The firefly torches, chandeliers, and reading lamps illuminated, so pale orange light filled the library. For several seconds, Cressida, Firefly, Moon, and Breeze stood quietly and admired the library. Cressida thought it looked like the best library she could imagine: it had even more books than her school's library, and certainly more than twelve were about unicorns.

Firefly looked at Cressida. "Thank you so very much for all your help. You saved the day once again."

"You're welcome," Cressida said. "Glow Library is the best library I've ever seen."

Just then, Cressida heard the clatter of hooves on the corridor leading to the library. She turned around as Sunbeam, Flash, Bloom, and Prism trotted through the door.

"Wow!" Sunbeam said. "I've never seen so many books in one place!"

"Those armchairs look even more comfortable than the ones in the front hall of Spiral Palace," Flash said.

"Those are the best firefly chandeliers I've ever seen," Prism said, admiring the ceiling.

"Welcome to Glow Library!" Firefly said.

Chapter Eight

Just then, more creatures from the Rainbow Realm began to file into the Glow Library and browse the books. A cluster of painted fairies that Cressida recognized from her adventures with Prism stood by the Art and Artists section and looked at books together. Ernest pulled out several books from the Magic section, sat down on the floor, and

began to read them—just the way Cressida had in her school library earlier that day. Three phoenixes looked at books in the Adventure section. And six gnomes Cressida recognized from the Enchanted Garden huddled together in the Gardening and Plants section.

For several seconds, Cressida and the unicorn princesses watched all the magical creatures browse the books. Then Firefly said, "Well, let's start reading!"

"I can't wait!" Bloom said. She hurried over to the Gardening and Plants section, chose a book, found an armchair, and plopped down.

Prism trotted over to the Art and Artists section. "I could spend weeks in here reading!" she exclaimed. "Well, I could as long as I could take breaks to paint. And," she added, smiling, "maybe to eat occasionally." She sat down in an armchair with a thick purple book.

"I never imagined there could be this many books about sports," Flash said, surveying the books in the Sports section. "Maybe I'll learn how to ice skate!" She pulled out a tall thin book, found the armchair closest to her, and began to read.

Sunbeam danced over to the Fun and Games section. "Here's a whole book about party games," she said, pulling out a yellow book. She hopped over to an armchair and began to read.

Moon trotted over to the fiction section

and pulled out a book. "Here's a book of stories about unicorns who live in a different realm," she said. "I can't wait!" She curled up on an armchair and began to read.

Breeze looked hesitant. She walked over to the Great Outdoors sections and stood for several seconds. Then her face brightened. "There's an entire book here just about kite flying," she said. "I'll give it a try!" She pulled out a blue book with a picture of three unicorns flying kites in a meadow on the cover. She shrugged, sat down in an armchair, and began to read.

Firefly looked at Cressida and smiled.

"How would you like to read *Adventures in the Air* together? We could share an armchair."

"I'd love that," Cressida said.

Cressida and Firefly looked around for the book the bookworms had made for Cressida. Firefly said, "I think when we were cleaning up we must have shelved your book." She trotted over to the Adventure section and pulled the book off the shelf. Then she hopped onto an armchair and left a space for Cressida. "Come on over!" Firefly said.

Cressida giggled and climbed onto the armchair, right next to Firefly. Firefly opened the book, and the two began to

read about a pink flying unicorn who traveled from realm to realm meeting fairies, magic reptiles, griffins, phoenixes, and other magical creatures.

👑

After Cressida and Firefly had finished reading the first five chapters of *Adventures in the Air*, Cressida felt her stomach rumble. And she had to admit, after spending so much time in the Glow Library thinking about books and reading books, she felt ready to get to work on her very own book.

"I'm having a great time reading with you," Cressida said to Firefly, "but I think I'd better go home and have a snack. Plus, I want to starting writing and illustrating my book about the Rainbow Realm."

"I thought I heard your stomach growling," Firefly said, smiling. "Why don't you take *Adventures in the Air* with you? You can bring it back whenever you're finished. After all, this is a library. The whole point is to borrow books!"

Cressida grinned at the possibility of

reading more about the flying unicorn's adventures that night before bed. But then she remembered that usually the clothes and gifts she received in the Rainbow Realm disappeared during her journey back to the human world. "Do you think I'll be able to bring it back with me?" Cressida asked.

"I'm not entirely sure," Firefly said, "but I think so. And it certainly won't hurt to try."

"Well, thank you!" Cressida said. She stood up and stretched. Then she put *Adventures in the Air* inside her backpack, zipped it up, and put it on.

Sunbeam, Flash, Bloom, Prism, and Moon all looked up from their books and smiled at Cressida. Breeze, however, was fast asleep, with her mouth stretched into an enormous grin.

"Thank you for coming!" Sunbeam and Flash called out.

"Come back soon!" Bloom said.

Prism and Moon held up their hooves to wave.

Then Moon turned toward Breeze and said, "Psst! Wake up! Cressida is leaving."

Breeze slowly opened her eyes and yawned. "I was having the best dream. It was all about flying kites and running through meadows." She grinned and winked at Cressida. "Come back soon!"

"Thank you so much, again, for saving the library," Firefly said. "This has been the best grand opening party I ever could have imagined. And by the way, I spotted your spell book in the Magic section. It's there waiting for you any time you need to borrow it."

"That sounds great," Cressida said. And then her stomach rumbled so loudly that all the unicorn princesses heard it and giggled. Cressida blushed and laughed along with them. She pulled her key from the back pocket of her jeans.

She wrapped her fingers around the handle of the key and said, "Take me home, please."

The Glow Library began to spin into a swirl of orange and yellow. Then everything went pitch black, and Cressida felt

Cressida grinned. She couldn't wait to go home and start drawing the cover of her first book, *The Rainbow Realm*. She slid her books into her backpack, zipped it up, and put it on. And then she skipped home, her silver unicorn sneakers blinking the whole way.

DON'T MISS OUR NEXT MAGICAL ADVENTURE!

TURN THE PAGE FOR A SNEAK PEEK . . .

In the top tower of Spiral Palace, Ernest, a wizard-lizard, stood in front of a full-length mirror. He straightened his pointy wizard's hat and furrowed his brow. He pushed his mouth into a straight line. And then he held up his wand as though he were about to cast a spell.

He froze and studied his reflection.

Then, he shook his head. "No, no, no," he whispered. "I look too serious."

He tilted his hat slightly. He widened his eyes and opened his mouth as though he were shouting. He lifted his wand. He paused for a few seconds, and then he sighed. "That's no good, either," he muttered. "I look too . . . enthusiastic."

Ernest began to push his hat backward when he heard a knock on the door. He jumped in surprise and called out, "Come in!"

The door opened with a creak. And there stood a unicorn with a glossy pink coat, a shiny pink mane, and a long pink tail. Around her neck, a ruby hung on a white ribbon necklace.

"Princess Feather!" Ernest exclaimed, dancing across the room. "You're back! What a wonderful surprise!"

Feather grinned. "Am I interrupting anything?" she asked.

"Oh no," Ernest said, straightening his cloak. "I was just, um, practicing different poses for casting spells."

Feather laughed. "I just returned from an amazing adventure in the Aqua Realm, the Witches' Realm, and the Reptile Realm. You are one of the first creatures in the Rainbow Realm I wanted to see."

"I've missed you," Ernest said.

"I've missed you too," Feather said. "In the Reptile Realm, I met some wizard-lizards who said you might be their distant cousin. And that made me miss you even more."

Ernest blushed. Then he smiled hopefully. "Now that you're back, you don't happen to need any magical assistance, do you?" he asked. "I've been practicing my magic while you were gone, and now I never make mistakes. Well, hardly ever. Actually, maybe occasionally. But really, I've gotten much better at it."

Emily Bliss lives just down the street from a forest. From her living room window, she can see a big oak tree with a magic keyhole. Like Cressida Jenkins, she knows that unicorns are real.

Sydney Hanson was raised in Minnesota alongside numerous pets and brothers. She has worked for several animation shops, including Nickelodeon and Disney Interactive. In her spare time she enjoys traveling and spending time outside with her adopted brother, a Labrador retriever named Cash. She lives in Los Angeles.

www.sydwiki.tumblr.com